For my ponies.
Thank you for always being there.
I love you. —BMV

BEATRIZ MARTIN VIDAL

BIRD

SIMPLY READ BOOKS

10:05

10:23

10:38   10:55

11:00

11:08

11:09

11:22

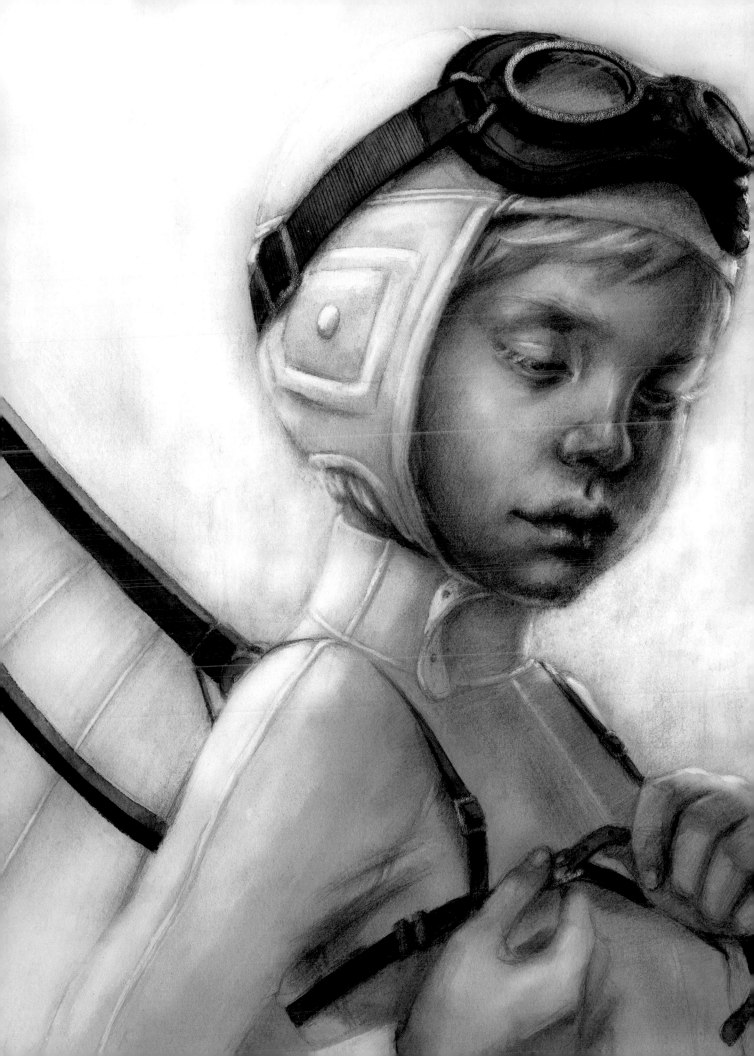

11:30

11:47

11:52

12:00

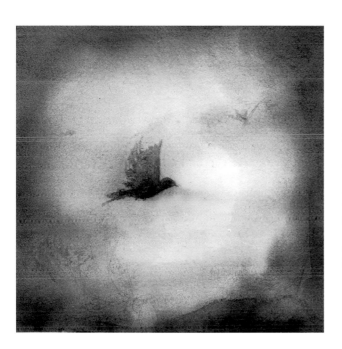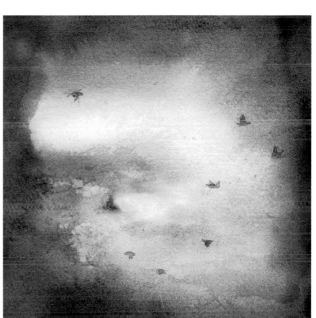

Published in 2015 by Simply Read Books
www.simplyreadbooks.com
Story and Illustrations © 2015 Beatriz Martin Vidal

Library and Archives Canada Cataloguing in Publication
Martin Vidal, Beatriz, artist
Bird / by Beatriz Martin Vidal.

ISBN 978-1-927018-64-4 (bound)

1. Stories without words. I. Title.

PZ7.M36827Bi 2015   j863'.7   C2014-906009-2

We gratefully acknowledge for their financial support of our publishing
program the Canada Council for the Arts, the BC Arts Council, and the
Government of Canada through the Canada Book Fund (CBF).

Manufactured in Italy
Book design by Naomi MacDougall

10 9 8 7 6 5 4 3 2 1